COPYRIGHT2021

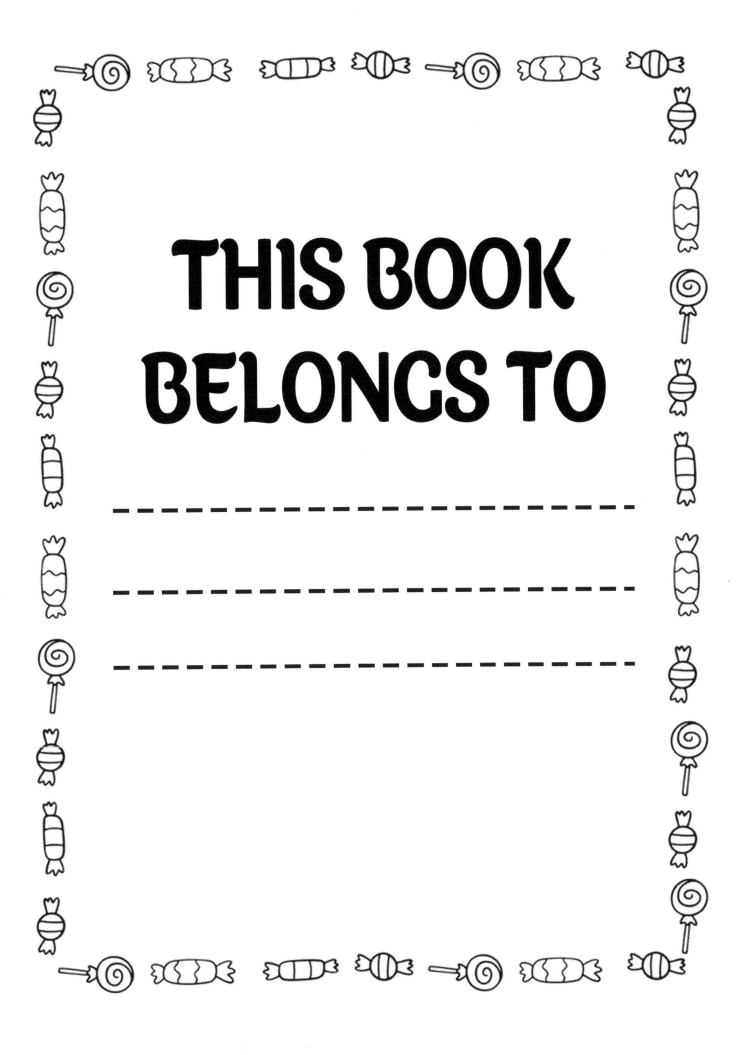

THIS BOOK BELONGS TO

A is for Apple

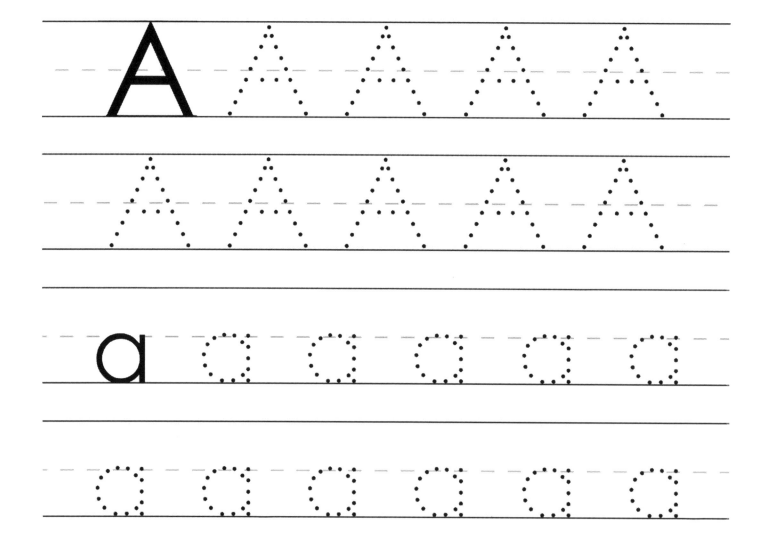

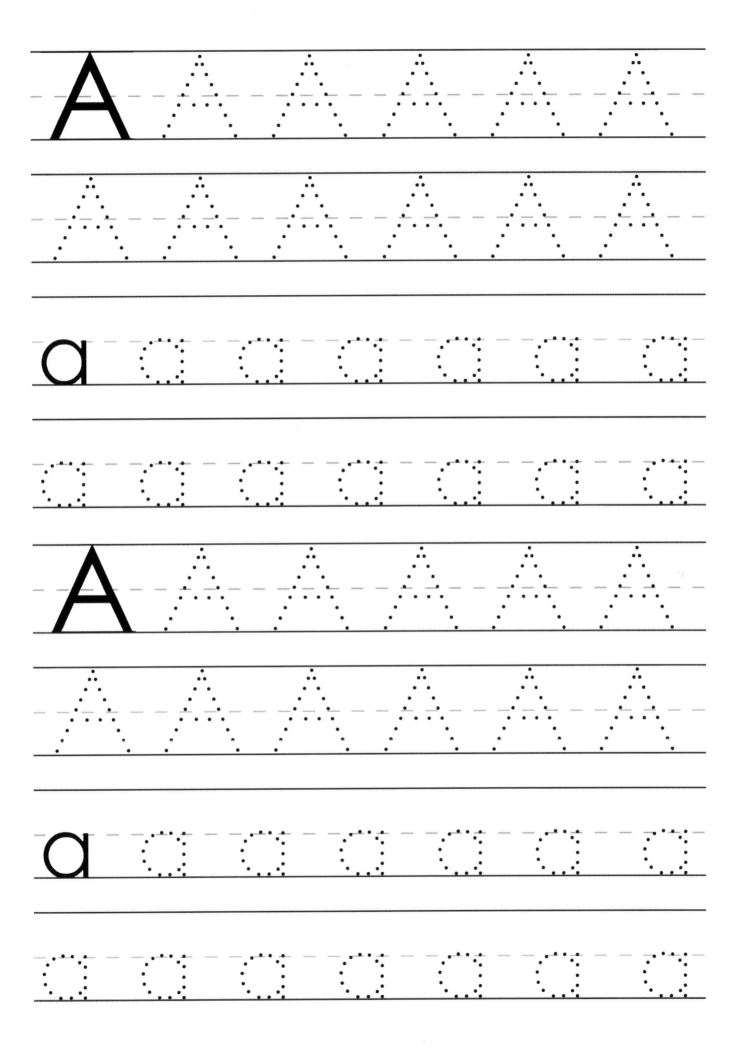

B is for Book

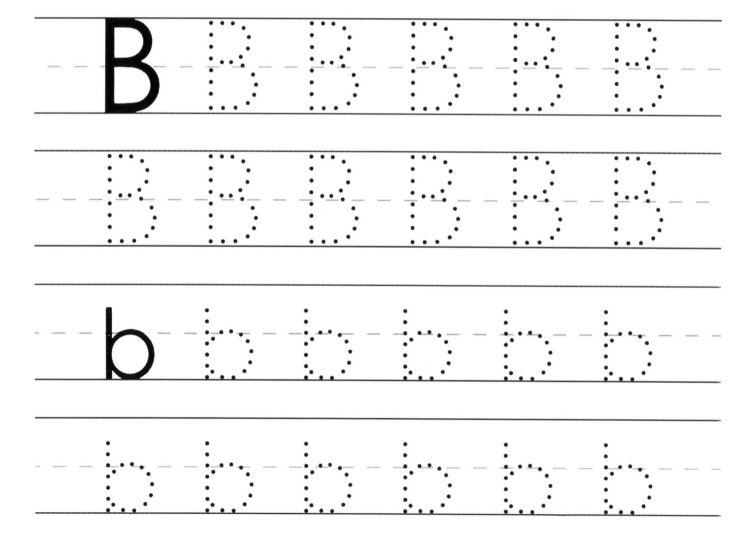

B B B B B B B

B B B B B B B

b b b b b b b

b b b b b b b

B B B B B B B

B B B B B B B

b b b b b b b

b b b b b b b

C is for Corn

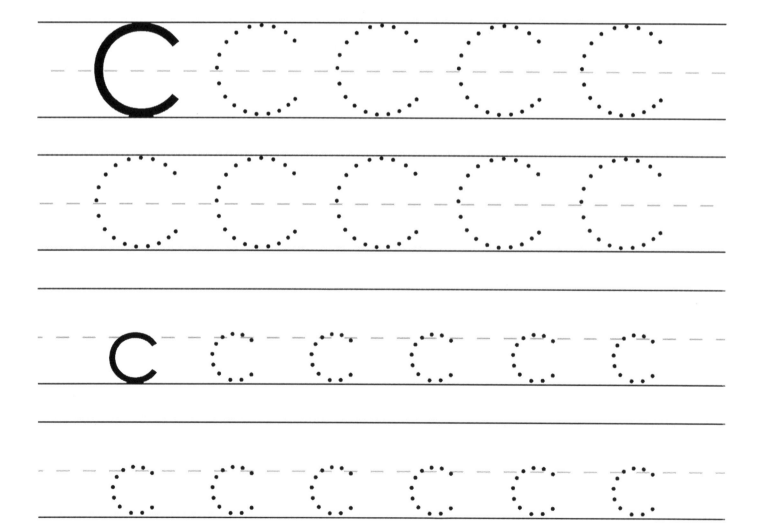

C C C C C C C C C C C

C C C C C C C C C C C C

C C C C C C C C C C C C C

C C C C C C C C C C C C C

C C C C C C C C C C C

C C C C C C C C C C C C

C C C C C C C C C C C C

C C C C C C C C C C C C

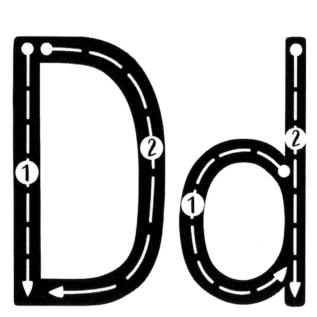

D is for Drum

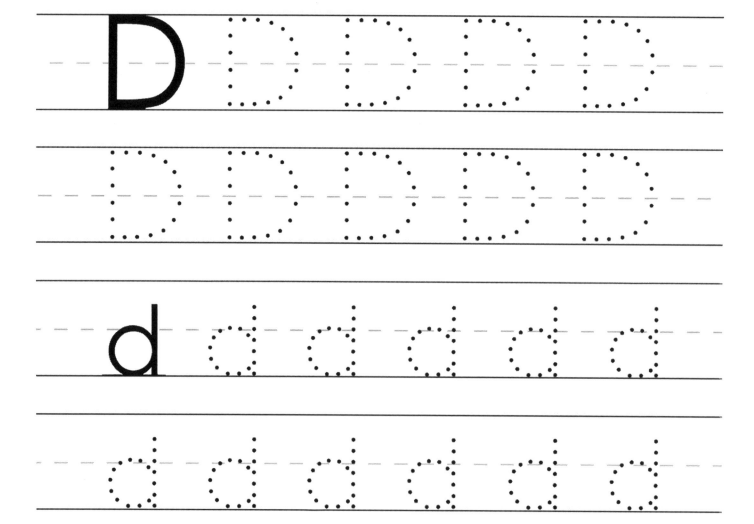

D

D

d

d

D

D

d

d

E is for Egg

E

e

F is for Flower

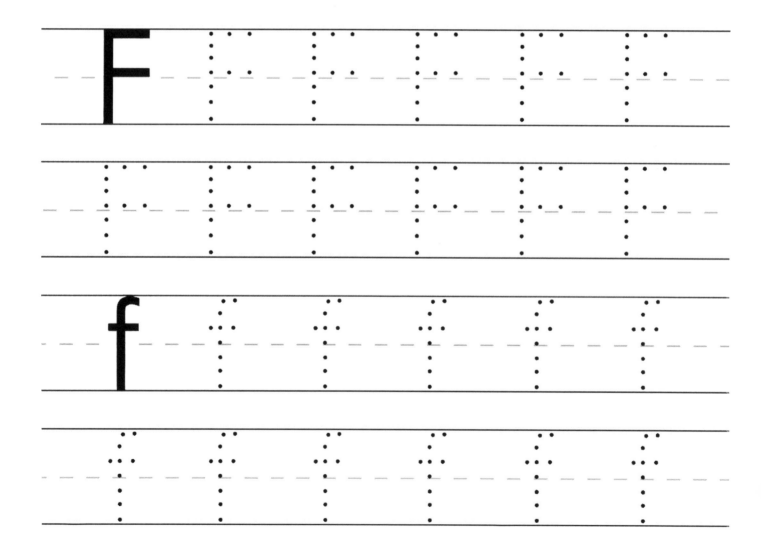

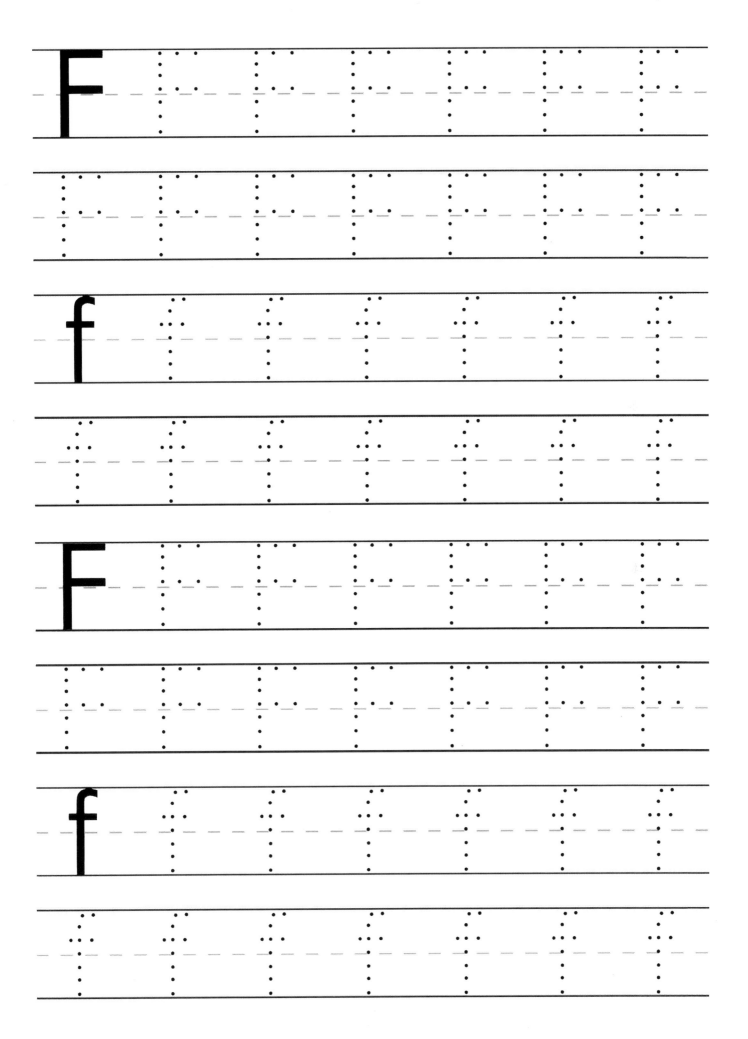

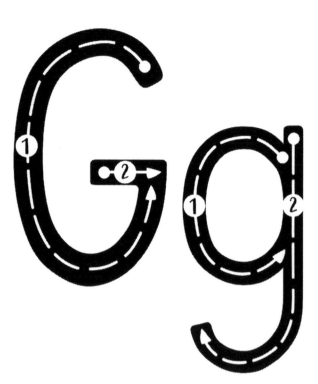

G is for Gift

G

g

G g

G G G G G G G G G G G

G G G G G G G G G G

g g g g g g g

g g g g g g g

G G G G G G G G G G G

G G G G G G G G G G

g g g g g g

g g g g g g

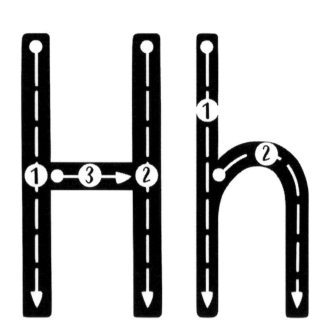

H is for House

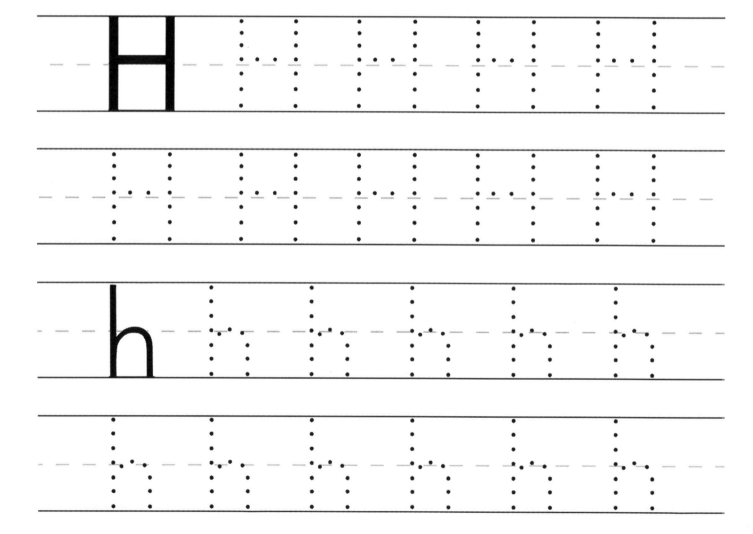

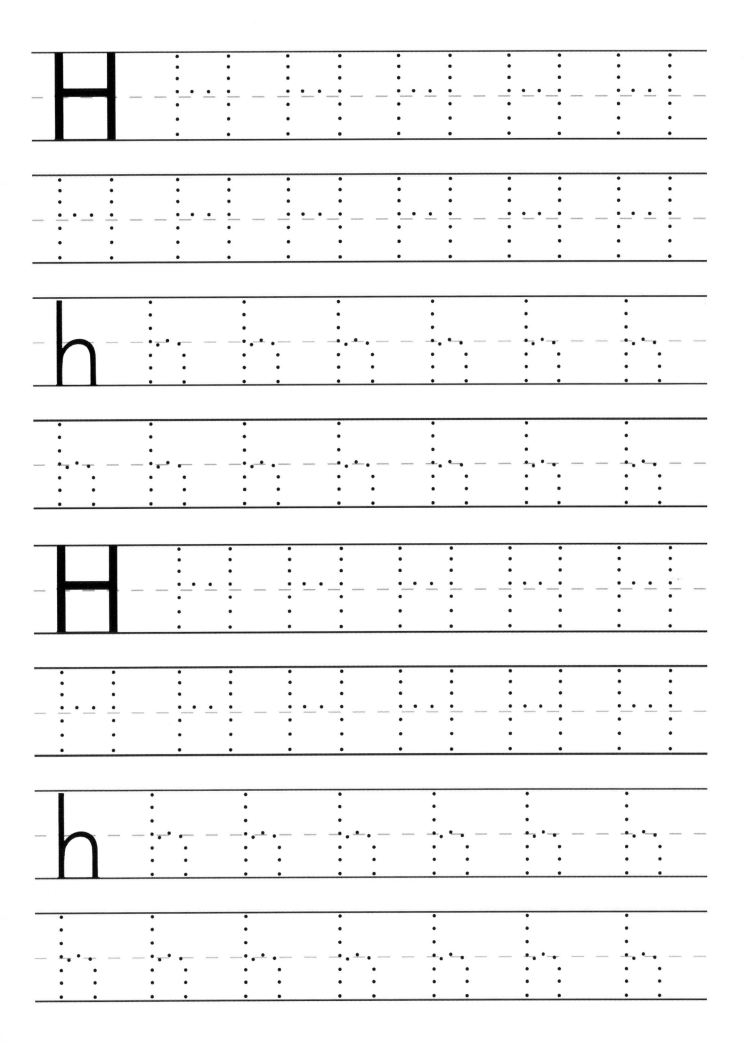

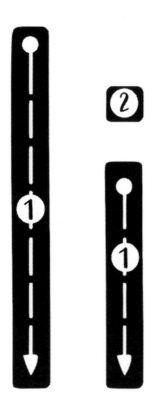

I is for Ink

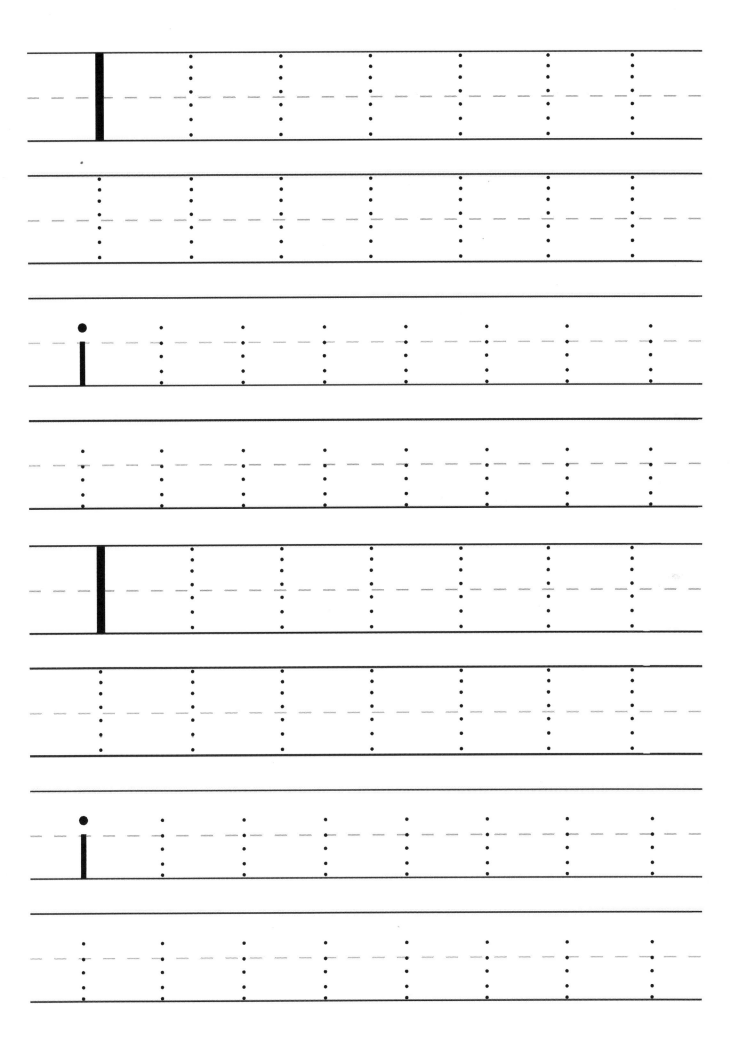

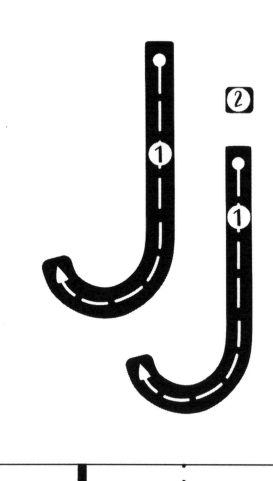

J is for Jam

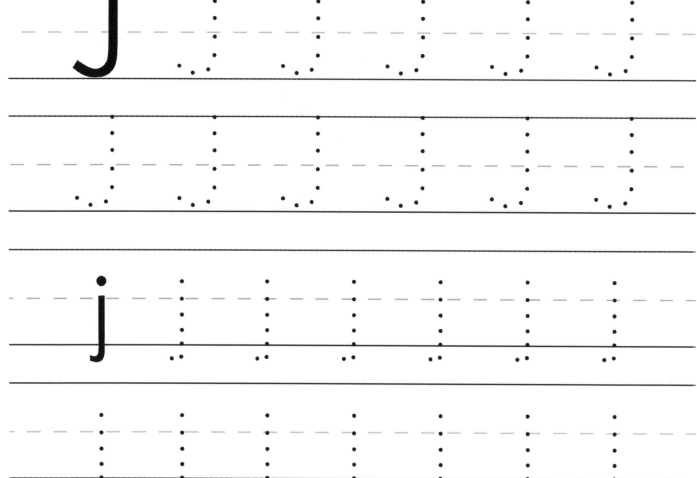

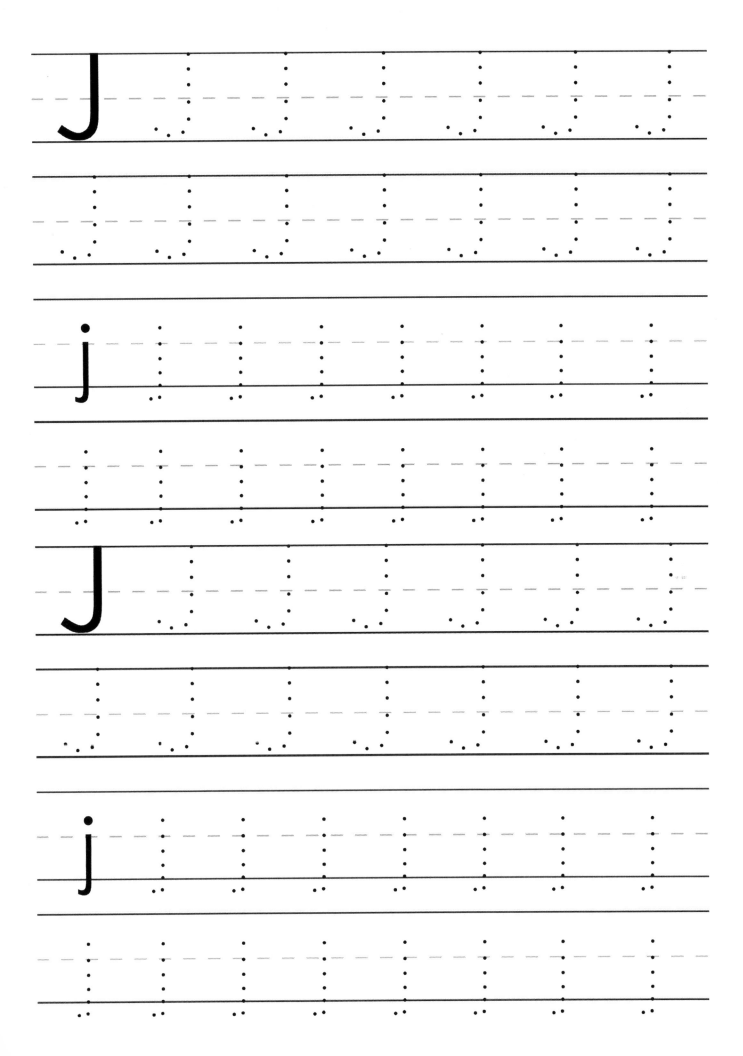

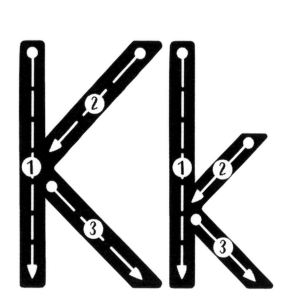

K is for Kettle

K k K K K K K K

K K K K K K K

k k k k k k k

k k k k k k k

K K K K K K K

K K K K K K K

k k k k k k k

k k k k k k k

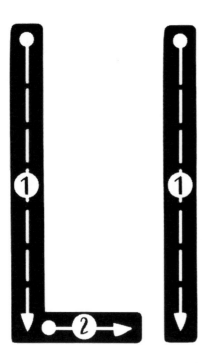 

L is for Letter

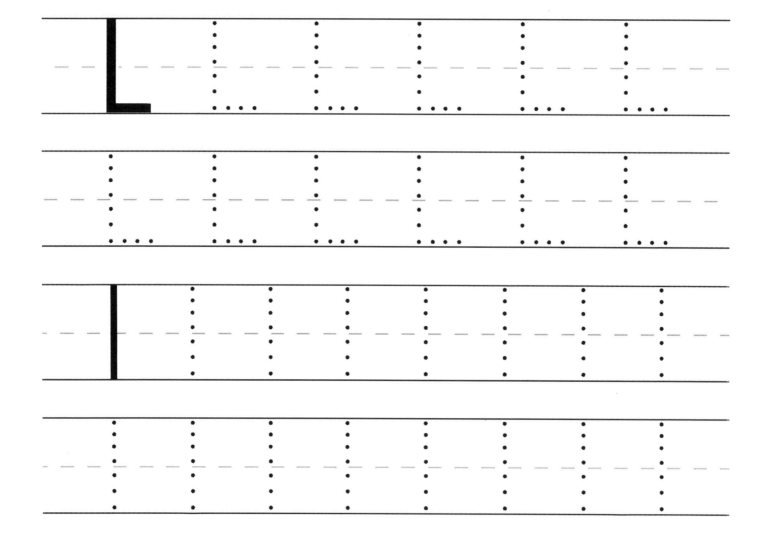

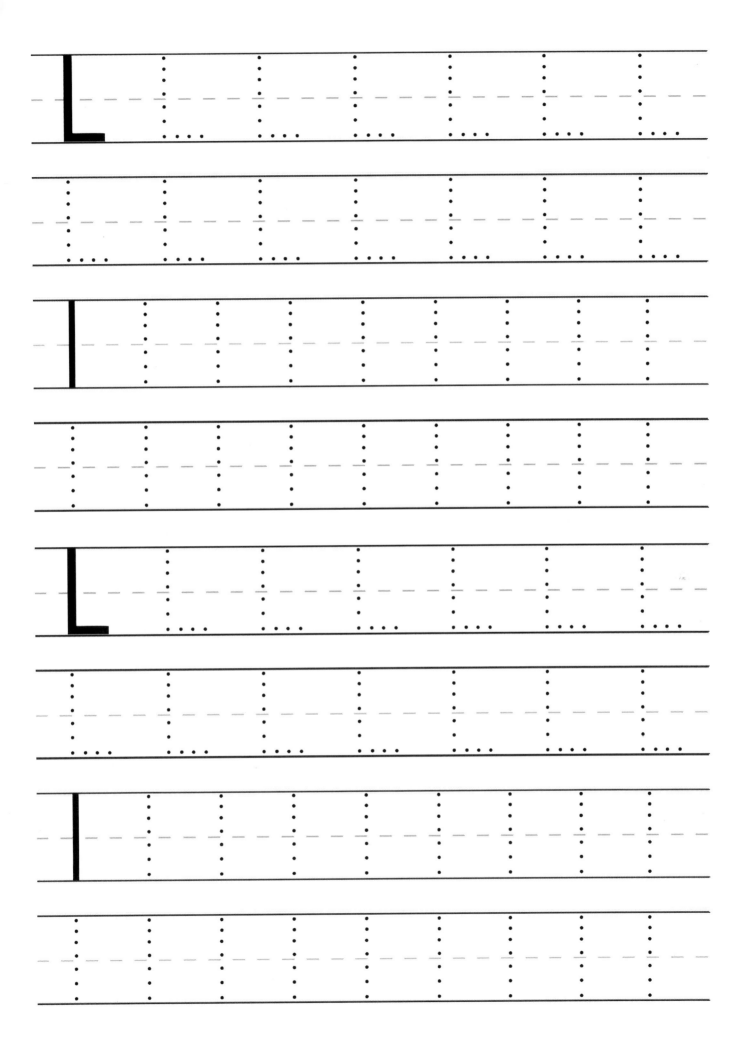

M is for Mirror

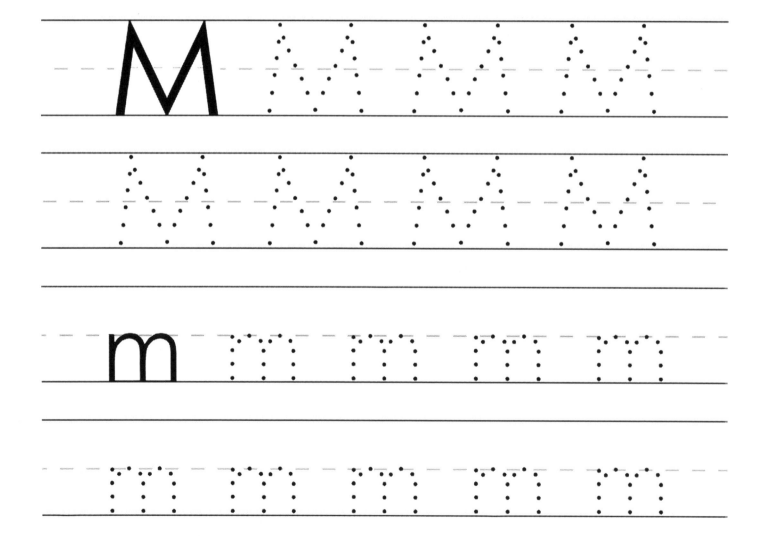

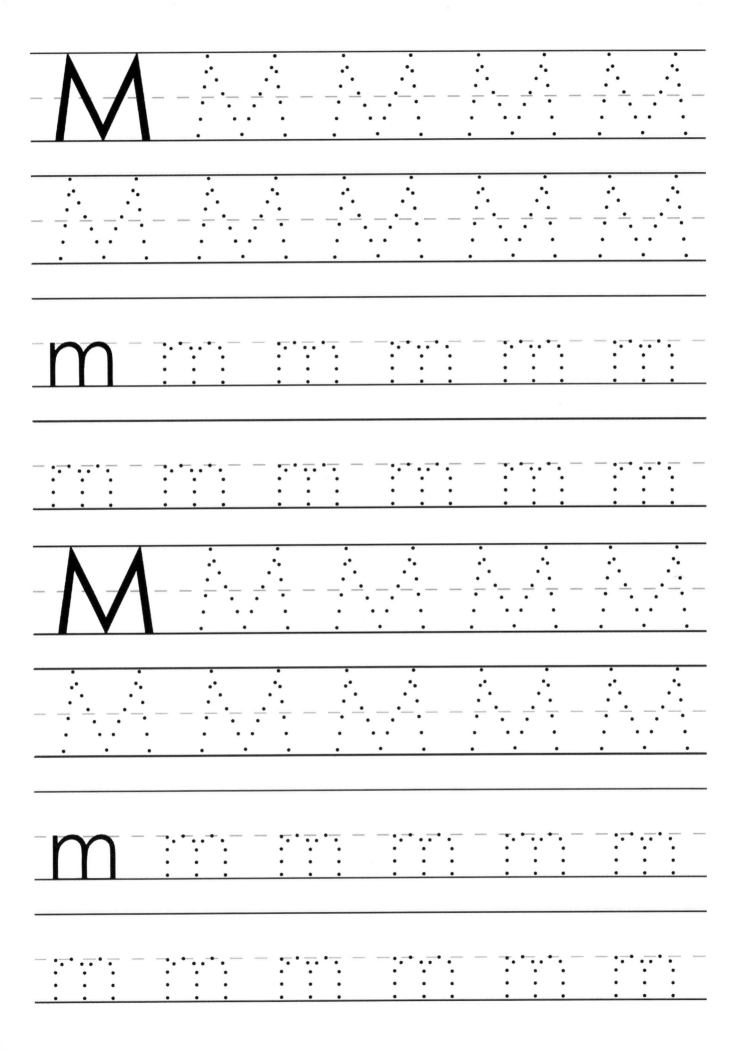

N is for Net

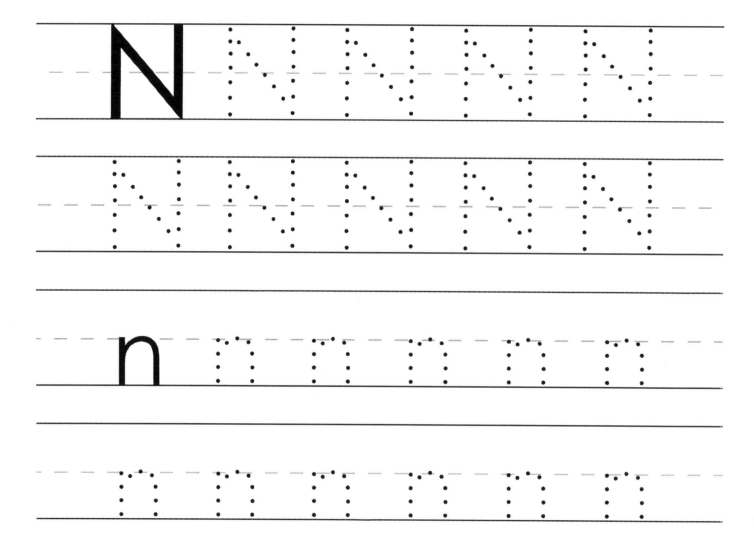

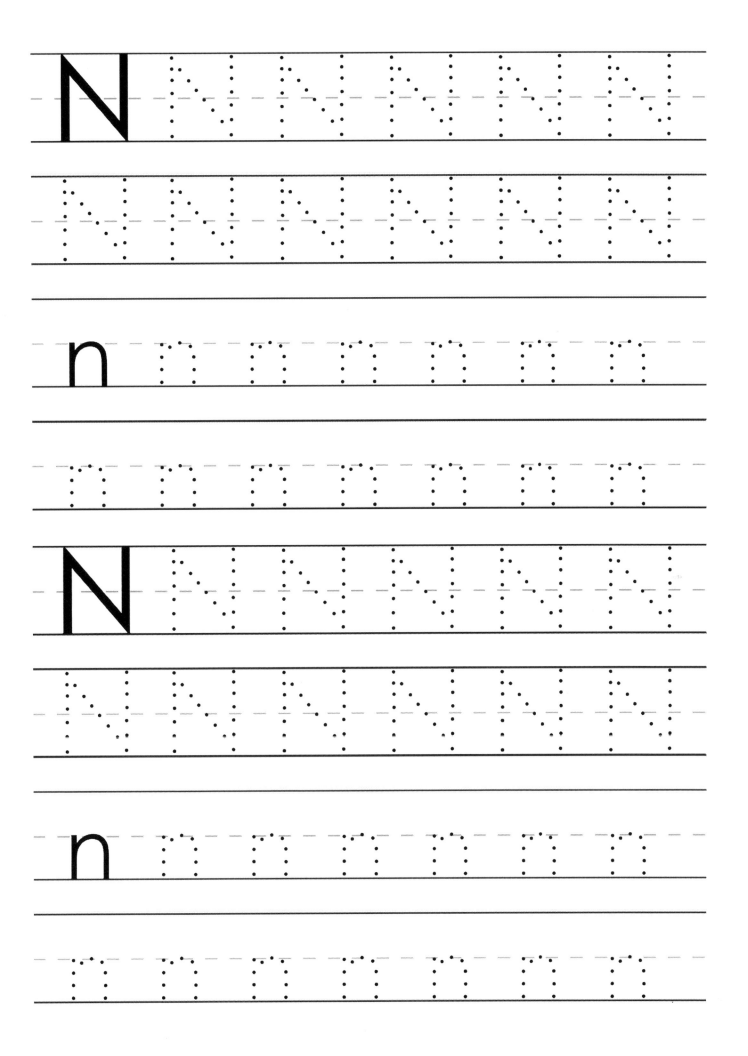

O is for Oven

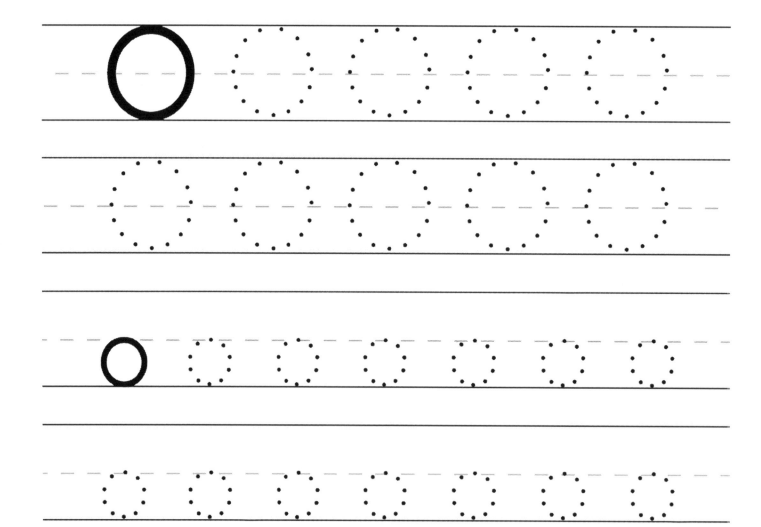

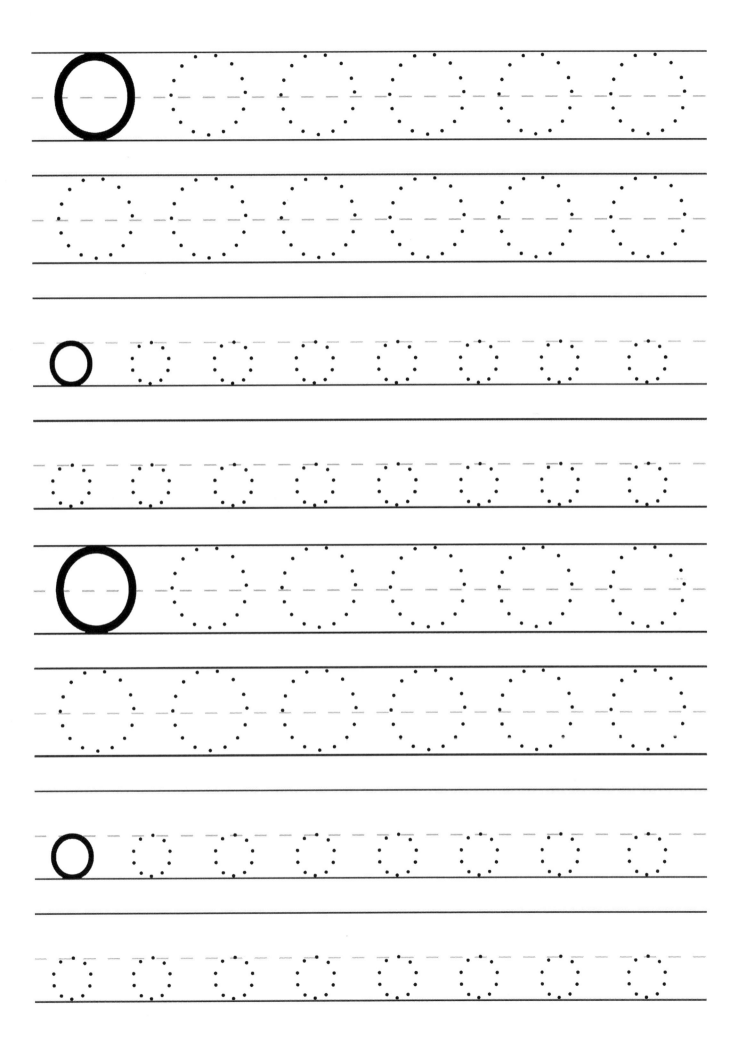

P is for Pineapple

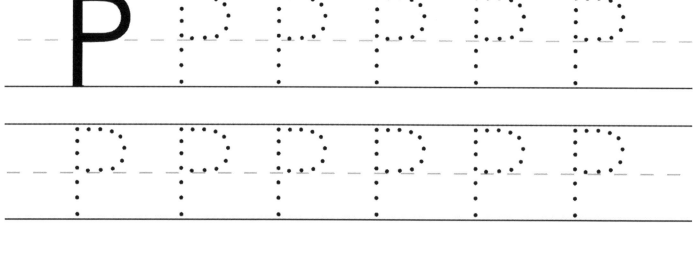

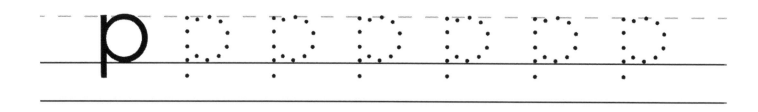

P P P P P P P P

P P P P P P P

p p p p p p p p

p p p p p p p

P P P P P P P P

P P P P P P P

p p p p p p p p

p p p p p p p p

Q is for Quartz

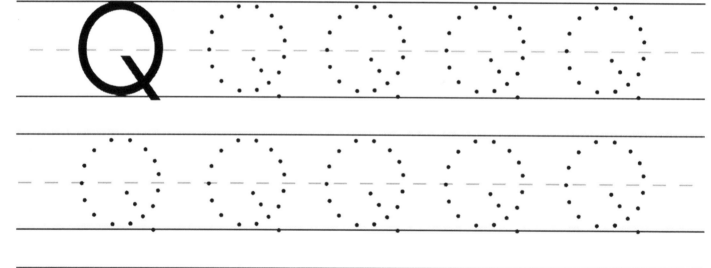

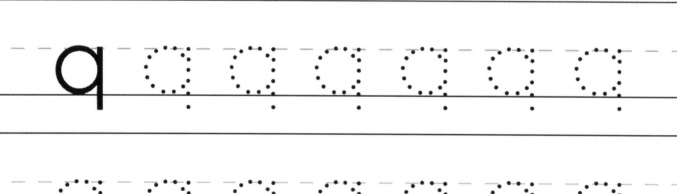

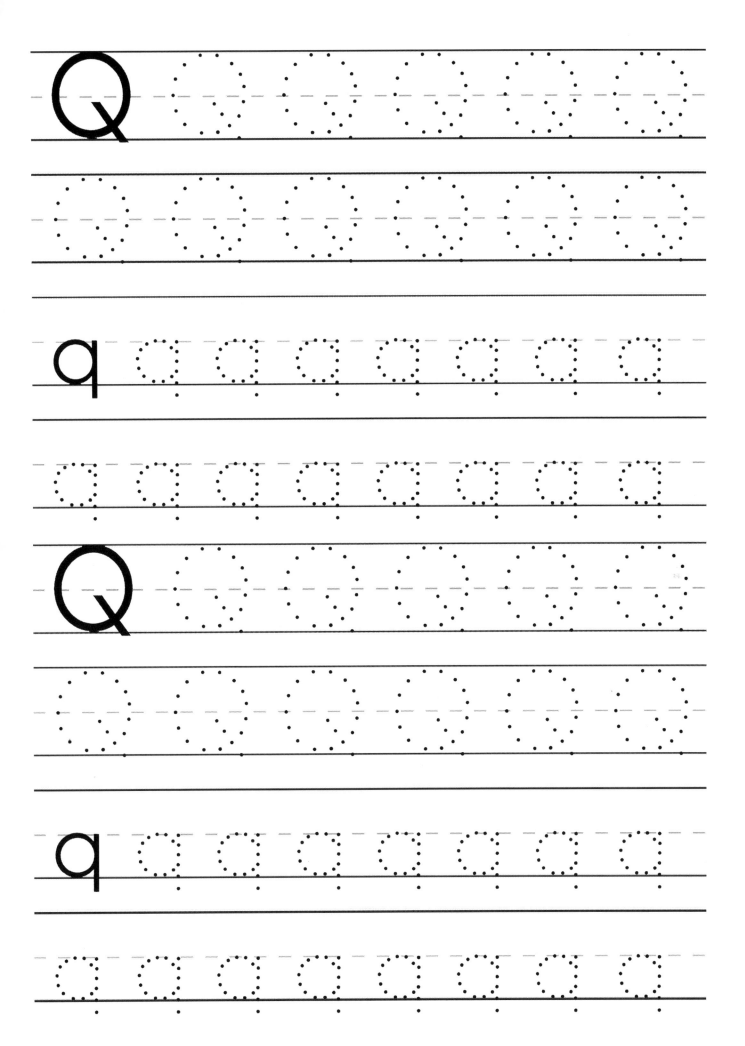

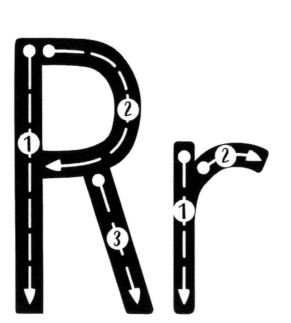

R is for Ring

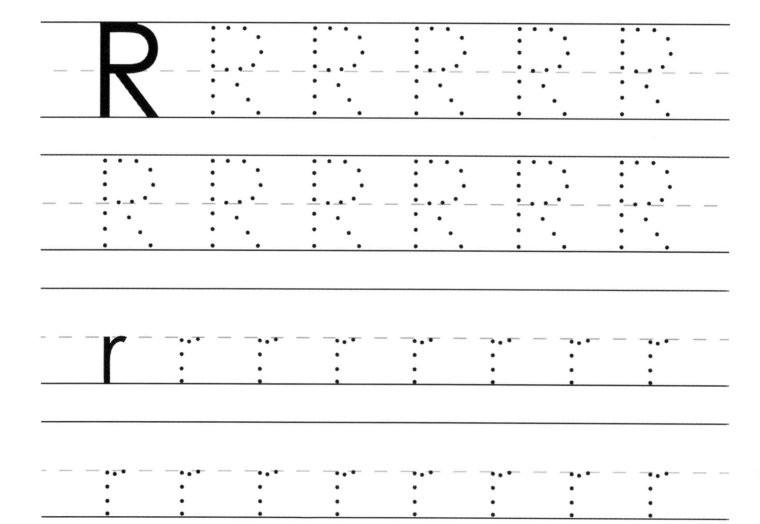

R R R R R R R R R

R R R R R R R R R

r r r r r r r r r

r r r r r r r r r

R R R R R R R R R

R R R R R R R R R

r r r r r r r r r

r r r r r r r r r

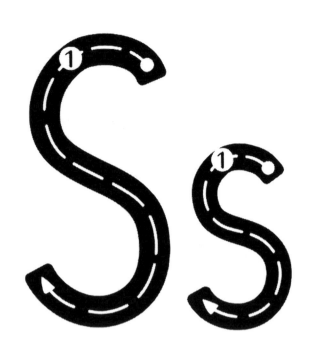

S is for Star

S

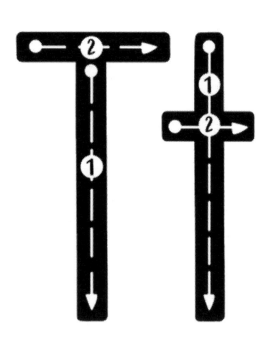

T is for Tomato

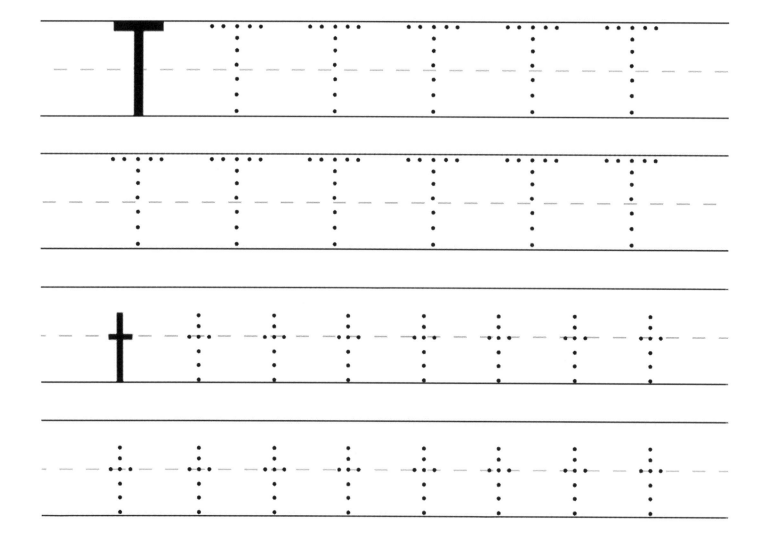

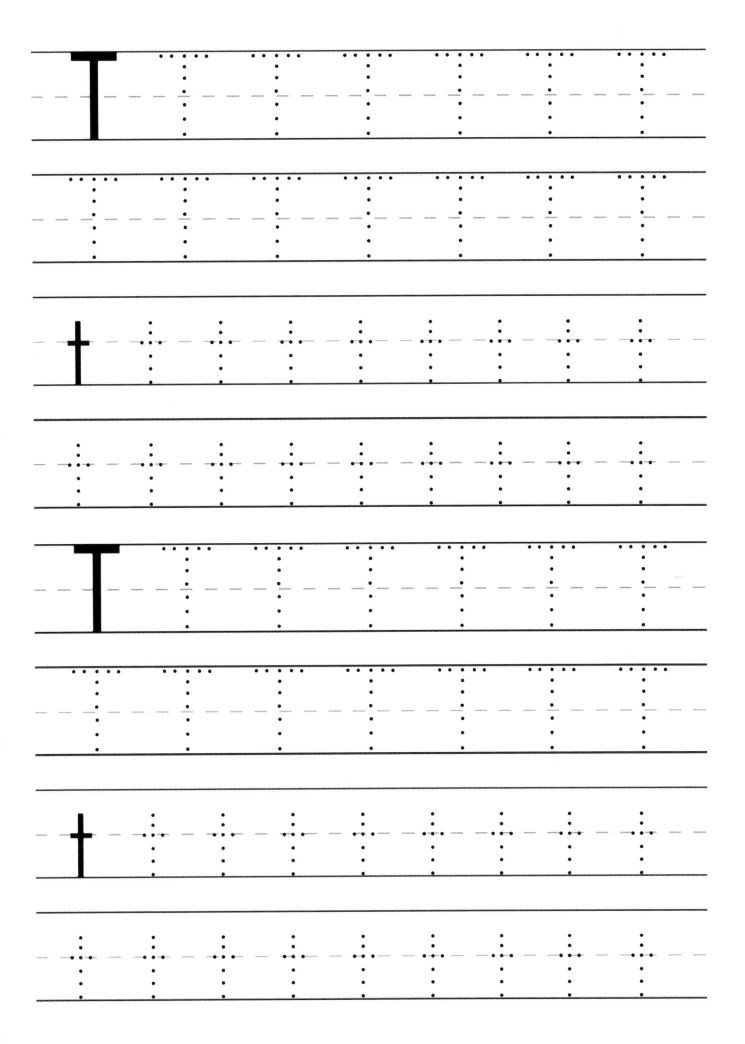

U is for Ugli Fruit

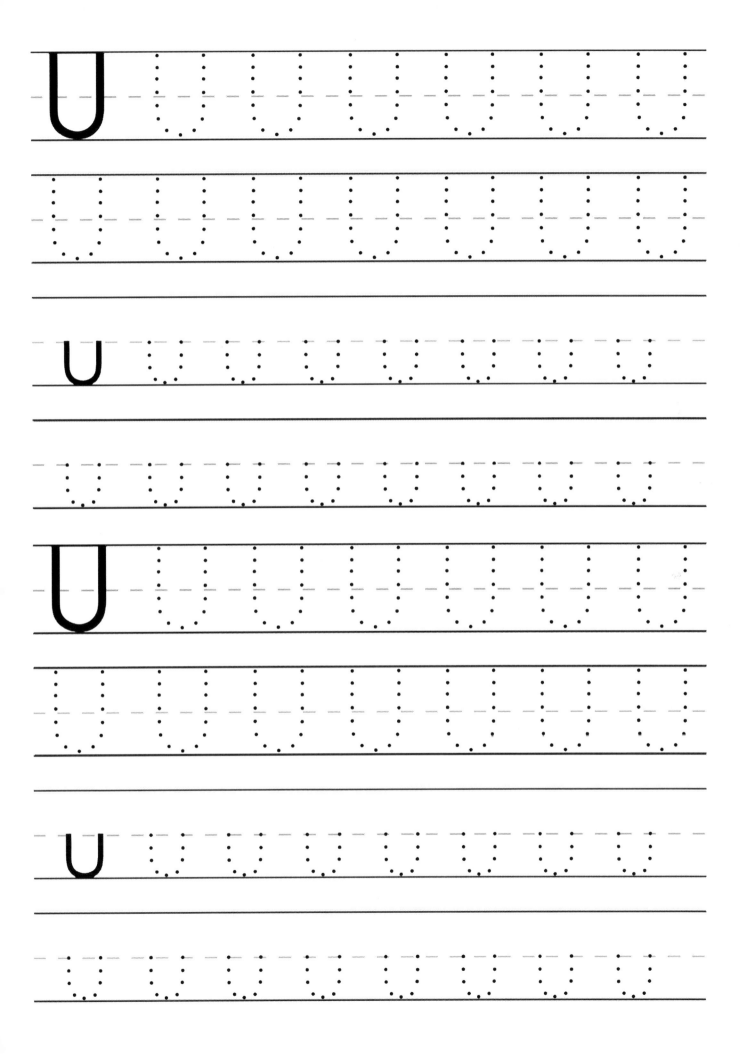

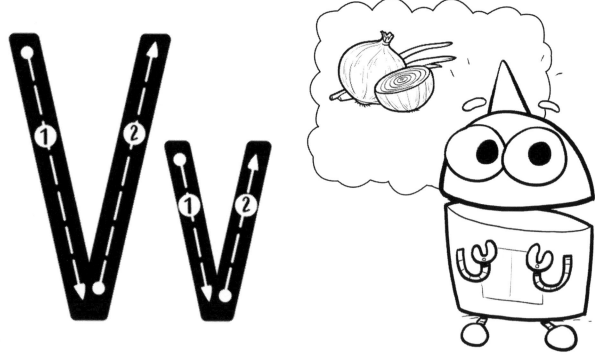

V is for Vidalia Onion

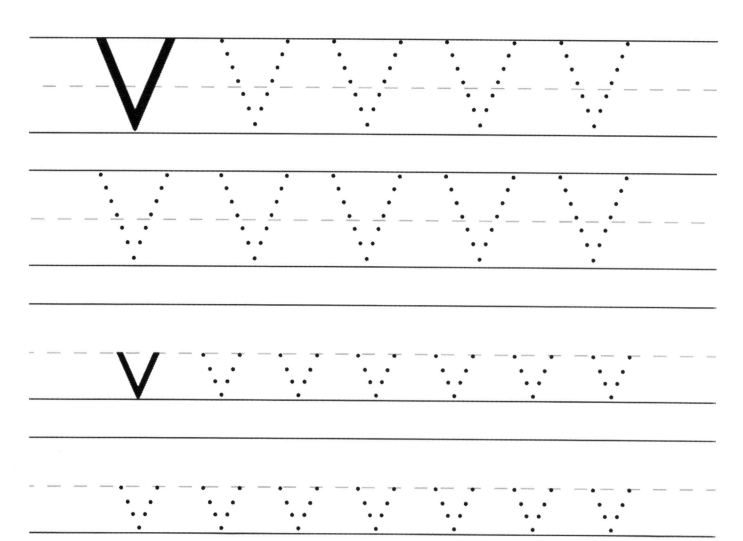

V V V V V V V V V

V V V V V V V V

V V V V V V V

V V V V V V V V

V V V V V V V V

V V V V V V V V

V V V V V V V

V V V V V V V

W is for Watch

W

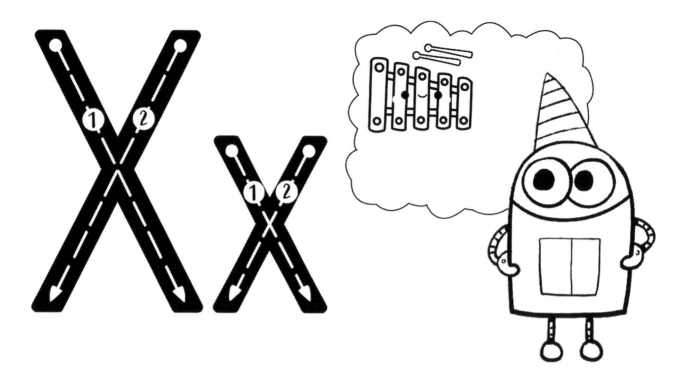

X is for Xylophone

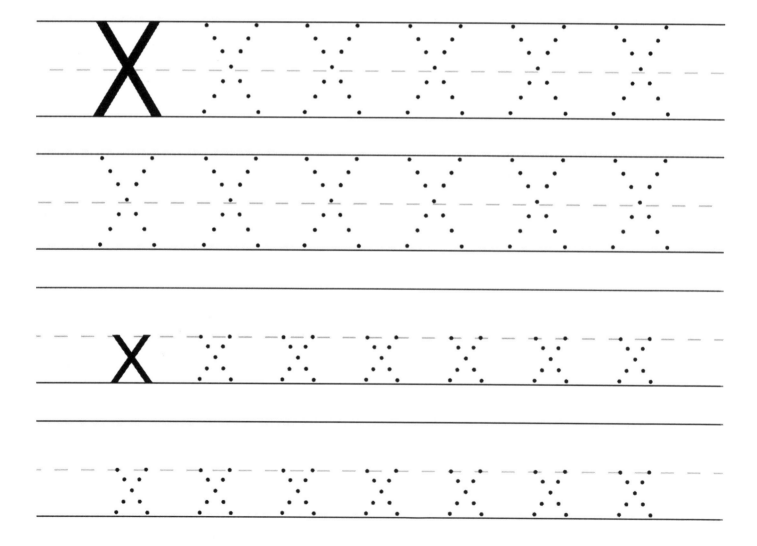

X

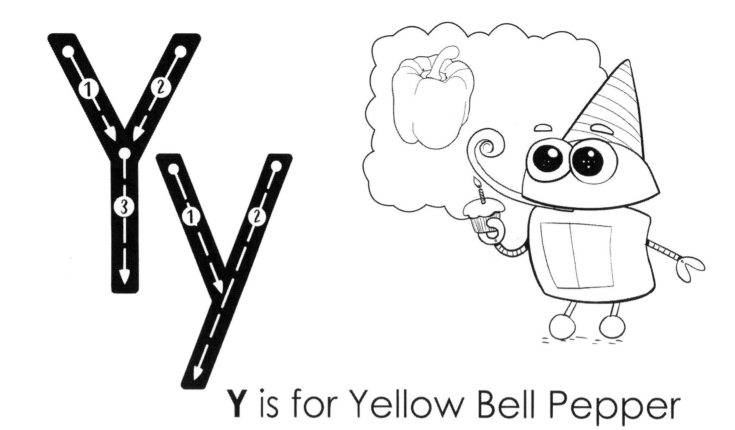

Y is for Yellow Bell Pepper

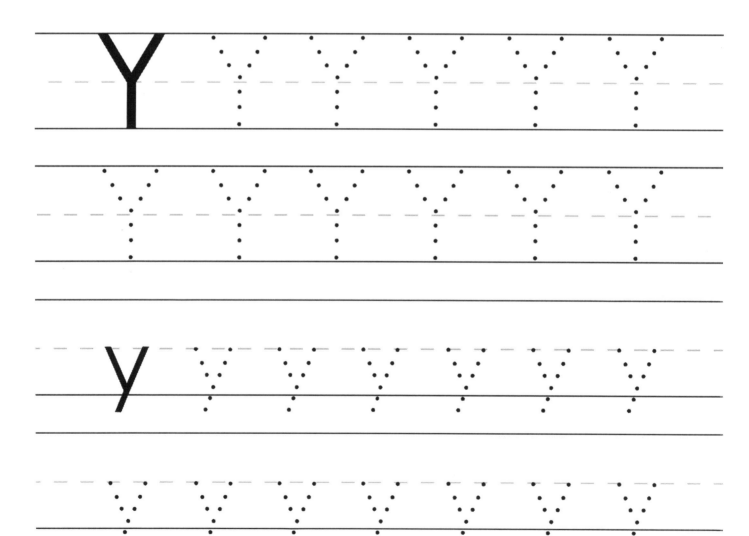

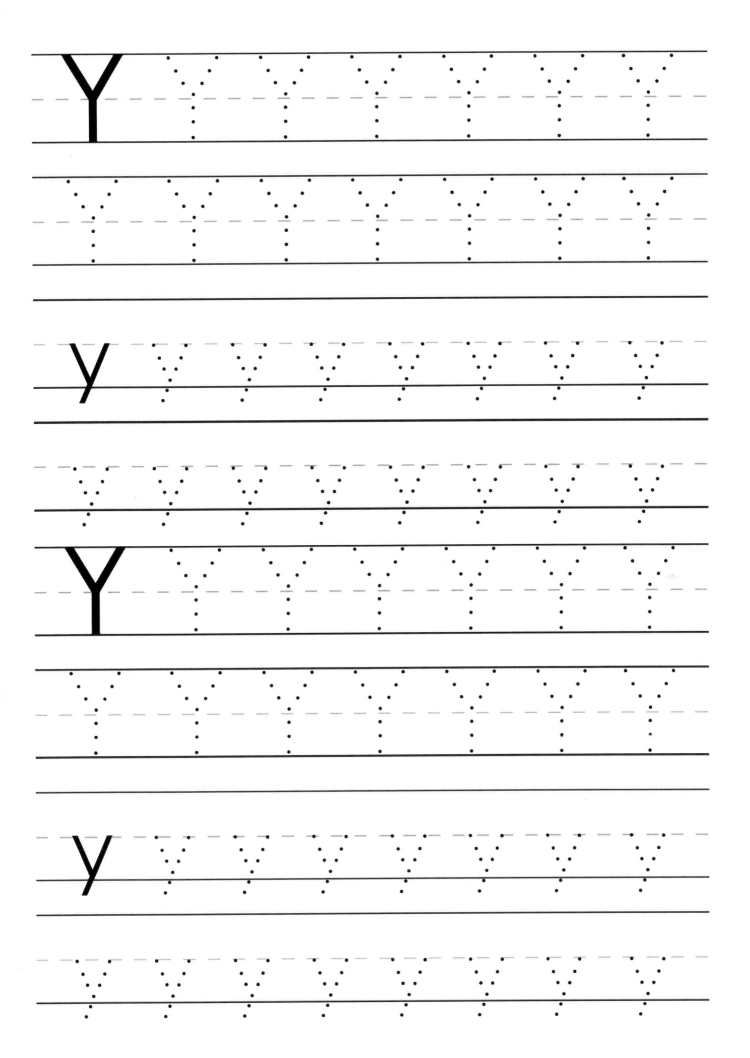

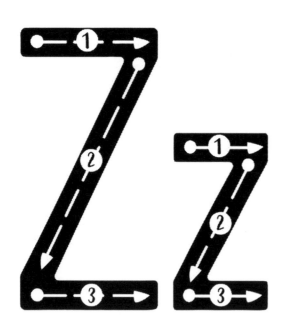

Z is for Zip

Z

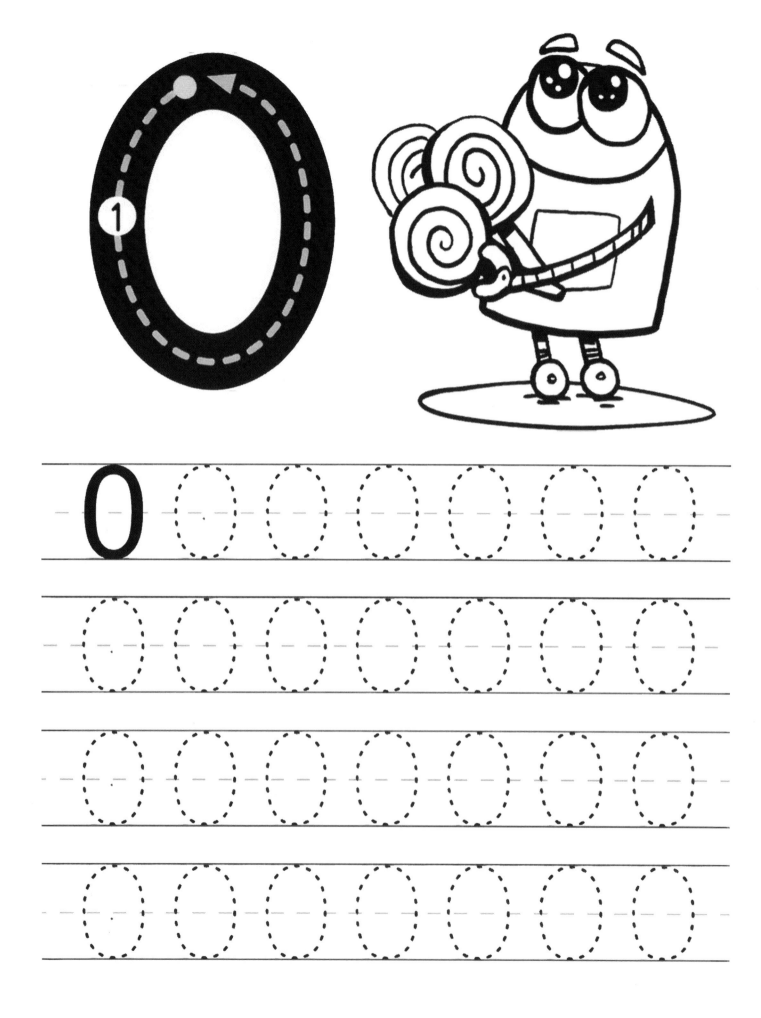

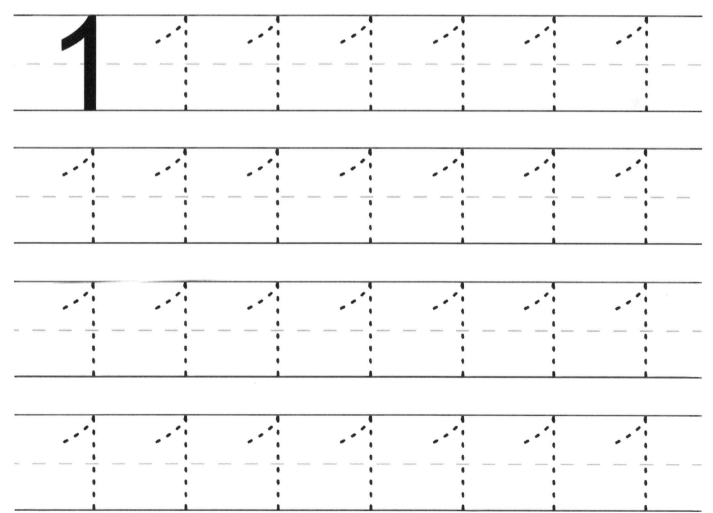

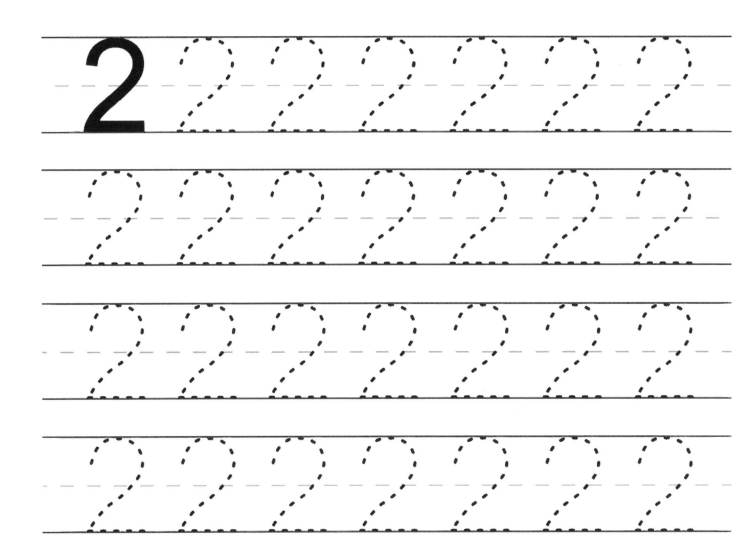

3 3 3 3 3 3 3

3 3 3 3 3 3 3

3 3 3 3 3 3 3

3 3 3 3 3 3 3

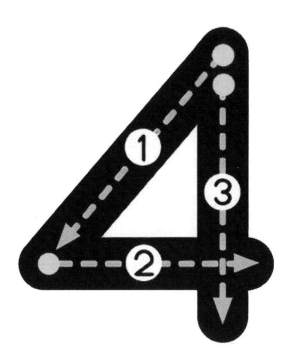

4

5 5 5 5 5 5 5 5

5 5 5 5 5 5 5

5 5 5 5 5 5 5

5 5 5 5 5 5 5

6 6 6 6 6 6 6

6 6 6 6 6 6 6

6 6 6 6 6 6 6

6 6 6 6 6 6 6

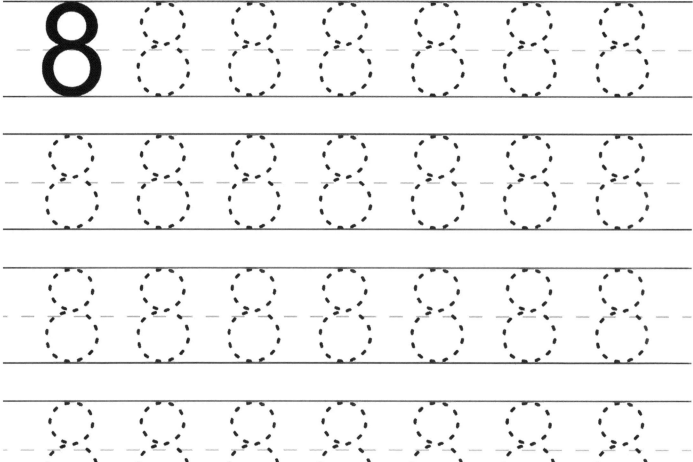

Happy Valentine's Day!

to:
from:

HAPPY VALENTINE'S DAY!

You're a

STAR!

to:
from:

BEE MY

FRIEND!!

STORYBOTS

Happy Valentine's Day!

to:
from:

HAPPY VALENTINE'S DAY!

You're a

STAR!

to:

from:

BEE MY

FRIEND!!

STORYBOTS

UR GR8

to:

from:

Happy
Valentine's Day!

to:

from:

HAPPY VALENTINE'S DAY!

TO:

FROM:

I think you're
tweet!

to:

from:

STORYBOTS

I THINK YOU'RE SWEET

to: from:

HAPPY
Valentine's
Day!

to:
from:

YOU'RE COOL

TO: FROM:

You're an awesome friend!

to:
from:

What tool did the worker need?

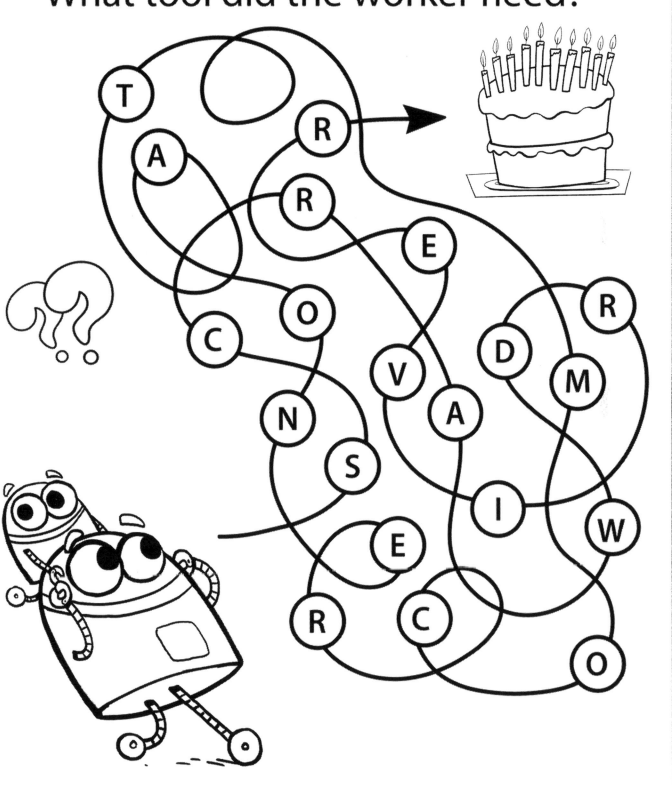

Spot 10 differences & color

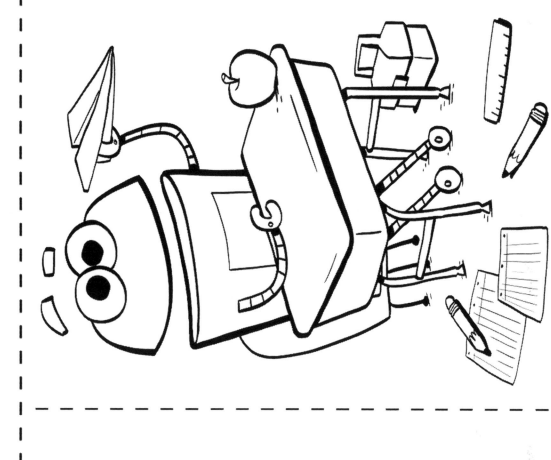

STORYBOTS

Bb

Trace the dotted lines to make the letter B!
Then write your own B next to it!

B b

B   B   B

b   b   b

Bb   Ball

STORYBOTS

Can you find all the patriotic words?
Circle them when you find them!

```
R  L  I  B  E  R  T  Y  A  X  J  D
X  M  I  S  W  O  M  X  S  J  P  E
S  T  R  I  P  E  S  K  L  P  N  B
Q  X  F  K  O  C  R  D  N  O  P  Q
I  C  Y  U  L  O  X  A  T  K  C  A
E  M  Q  E  W  T  R  G  C  M  D  M
I  N  D  E  P  E  N  D  E  N  C  E
S  B  R  J  T  I  C  J  P  S  J  R
I  I  X  E  H  P  V  S  H  G  I  I
F  X  V  S  T  A  R  S  Q  U  Y  C
R  P  A  T  R  I  O  T  I  C  D  A
A  W  O  F  L  A  G  S  B  O  O  M
```

Patriotic   Flag   Stars   Stripes

Boom   America   ~~Liberty~~

Cut and color. Flashcards

Bb

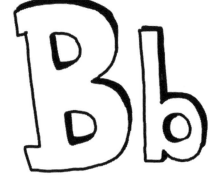

Can you find all the words
that start with **B**?
Circle them when you find them!

B (B U T T O N) B X
X A Y D L X B U U
B L S L W E M T F
R R A E A Z A T G
B B E R B N A E L
I B B A A A M R Z
R A O N D L L F F
D T A A U Y T L R
J B T B A L L Y A

Butterfly	~~Button~~	Bear	Boat	Bat
Banana	Bread	Bird	Baseball	Ball

Cut and color. Flashcards

Cc

Connect the dots in **alphabetical** order to make a **sea creature** that starts with the letter **C.**

Color it when you're done!

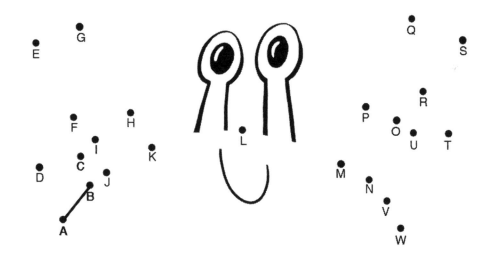

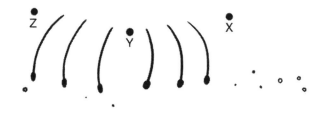

"I live under rocks and I have pincers. Snap Snap! I'm a _____"

STORYBOTS

Heart Garland

Supplies!

A Long Strip of Paper
(Any size will work,
but you could try 3 inches by 17 inches.)

Pencil

Scissors

Fold one edge
of the strip of paper.

Keep folding like an accordion,
until you have a small folded square.

1 inch

Using a pencil, mark out
the edges of your heart,
being careful to leave an inch
of the edge connected.

Cut out your heart shape,
being sure to leave
a segment of the edge clear.

Unfold your heart,
and you have a great garland!

The StoryBots present: **Pink Lemonade**

Supplies

10 Lemons

Sugar (1 cup)

Water (2 cups)

Cranberry Juice (1/2 Cup)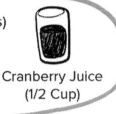

Juice your lemons.

Add the lemon juice and sugar to a pitcher.

Mix until all the sugar is dissolved!

Add your water and cranberry juice, and mix well!

2 cups water

1/2 cup cranberry juice

Share with your friends and family.

Heart Garland

Supplies!

A Long Strip of Paper
(Any size will work,
but you could try 3 inches by 17 inches.)

Pencil

Scissors

Fold one edge
of the strip of paper.

Keep folding like an accordion,
until you have a small folded square.

1 inch

Using a pencil, mark out
the edges of your heart,
being careful to leave an inch
of the edge connected.

Cut out your heart shape,
being sure to leave
a segment of the edge clear.

Unfold your heart,
and you have a great garland!

Color and cut out these bookmarks
to help you keep your place in any book!

STORYBOTS

HOW TO:

Make a paper bag StoryBot

STORYBOTS®

Supplies!

Paper Bag

Plain White Paper

Construction Paper

Scissors

Plate

Marker

Glue

Using a paper plate as your guide,
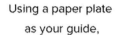
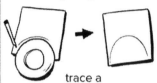
trace a half circle out of your construction paper.

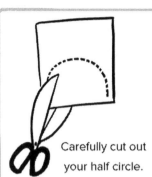
Carefully cut out your half circle.

Cut out two small circles
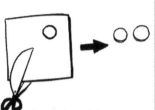
from the white paper.

Lay your paper bag down with the flap facing up.

Carefully glue your half circle onto the flap.

Glue the white circles onto the half circle.
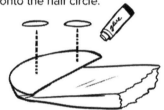
Those are the eyes!

With a marker, draw some pupils for your StoryBot.

Lay your bag on a sheet of construction paper.
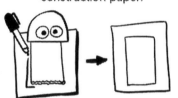
Trace around it!

Cut out the rectangle you made!

Fold it in half.

Make two cuts where marked,
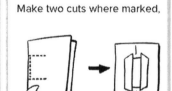
and then cut along the edge.

Glue it to the front of your bag.

This is your StoryBot body!

You can draw something special to go inside your StoryBot.

Now you have a StoryBot puppet!

Help the StoryBot deliver a valentine to his friend!

Help the leprechaun
get to his pot of gold!

The StoryBots Present:

Chocolate Fudge Truffles

Melt one (12 ounce) bag of chocolate chips!

You can use the microwave! On medium heat, zap it for 30 seconds at a time, until the chips are nice and mushy.

Careful, it's HOT!

Sweetened Condensed Milk (3/4 cup)

Vanilla Extract (1 tsp)

Mix until well blended.

Cover and put in the fridge for one hour.

Or until it's firm!

Using your hands, form the chocolate into balls (about an inch in diameter) or into any shape.

Roll in powdered sugar or sprinkles!

Eat them right away, or keep them in the fridge!

nom!

STORYBOTS

Can you find all the back to school words?
Circle them when you find them!

```
N A X S C H O O L C O A
W V A Y I W B B R Y T X
R V L Y I I L Z E O O Z
I A K U L V A X C E I W
T R N N H T T K E U D B
E L E B O O K S S L E S
N B M A K T M K S V S C
G C A K D I S E J Y K S
U R V G Z M U R W P V D
(T E A C H E R) T A O E F
D K R L P K B F A Q R B
C E T A P P L E V C C K
```

Apple   Homework   Books   Bag   Desk

Recess   School   ~~Teacher~~   Read   Write

HOW TO:

MAKE GINGERBREAD STORYBOTS

Gingerbread Dough

Icing

Candies

STORYBOTS™

ROLL out your dough.

CUT out your dough in a StoryBot shape.

Like this!

BAKE your gingerbread according to the recipe.

Let the cookies COOL

for an hour or so!

Prepare your icing and decorations!

Decorate your cookies!   You can make eyes, mouths, and arms!   Try using lots of different candies!

Let your icing dry!

Enjoy!

This book
belongs to:
_____

This book belongs to:
_____

From the library of:
_____

From the library of:
_____

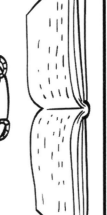

Cut and color these book plates
to label your books!

FIND THE RIGHT PATH

STORYBOTS®

Can you find all the birthday words?
Circle them when you find them!

```
O  C  O  N  F  E  T  T  I  H  A  T
S  U  R  P  R  I  S  E  Y  H  X  P
Q  L  X  M  A  Y  Y  F  Y  E  A  R
Z  J  T  N  W  D  J  Y  I  A  H  E
S  V  X  V  Q  X  M  Q  Y  L  A  S
C  P  Z  D  V  F  T  U  K  G  P  E
G  O  P  X  S  D  U  M  F  F  P  N
P  H  N  X  K  A  N  C  G  A  Y  T
C  A  Z  I  H  Y  J  C  A  K  E  W
V  Q  Y  Q  N  C  A  N  D  L  E  T
C  B  I  R  T  H  D  A  Y  M  Z  S
R  H  W  N  D  V  N  Z  V  R  L  W
```

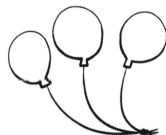

BIRTHDAY	CAKE	CANDLE	YEAR
PRESENT	HAPPY	~~CONFETTI~~	SURPRISE

Printed in Great Britain
by Amazon

72274358R00063